Chimes: A Monologue

Chimes: A Monologue

Tom Cole

The Song Cave

The Song Cave
www.the-song-cave.com

Layout by Kit Schluter

ISBN: 979-8-9931811-3-4
Library of Congress Cataloguing-in-Publication Data has been applied for.

FIRST PRINTING

Chimes: A Monologue

Finally, when everyone who could leave has left, and all the revelers are shamed out of the city, finally gone, there is for the first time quiet, finally quiet, on my block.

As this dawns on me, I begin to hear a chime out of the corner of my ear, light at first. I wonder, is it coming from inside my apartment? I check the drawers for devices gone bad—but as the week progresses the wind gets stronger, stronger, and the chime louder and louder until it is all I can hear and it is now clear the sound is coming from outside my apartment. Although other sounds are louder, it is the chime I hear, driving me crazy, deranged even. I go outside, against my better judgment (at that point none of us had masks), and find the culprit—a wind chime on a fire escape two buildings down. I look up at it, enraged. If I could only knock it down. Rocks?

I think about shooting it down with a gun.

I get a testosterone shot.

A simple wind chime, as wind chimes go—five hollow metal rods circling a ceramic disk in the center—a UFO.

A photographer friend who lives in that building agrees to knock on their door and ask them to take it down. I am grateful she is willing to take her life into her own hands in order to have contact with another human on behalf of a sound that is triggering to me. But they are gone, fled the city to their second home in the Hamptons out of fear, and this makes me hate them even more—their mobility offends me, as does their lack of consideration for neighbors. Or even worse, I think having a wind chime on your fire escape on a crowded city block is nothing but a hostile act against your neighbors.

What are they thinking? *Of course everyone enjoys the sounds of my wind chime as much as I do. I am doing my neighbors a service by giving them the peace I feel when I listen to my wind chime.* If I had the Lasso of Truth, I could somehow snag it, drag it down. But the more I look at the wind chime, and I can hardly do anything but look at it when I walk by, I see it is hung with strong rope and a thick knot. This isn't going to be easy. I think about calling 311.

It's an irritating remnant to the people who have to stay as they have fled an unpleasant situation, an indelible trace of their existence. All of this is driving me crazy, and I don't know if it is the wind chime, but I wonder, am I sick?

I'm feeling my glands and if I do catch it, I worry, who will take care of my dogs? Are they surfaces? One of them is epileptic. And blind in one eye. And has IBS. Who's going to deal with that? I shouldn't have gone to the gym that day. I'm checking my temperature every fifteen minutes. And there is something about the number fifteen that reminds me of those HIV tests from the '90s. To avoid the clinic, I'd spend $109 dollars at the drug store on a kit kept behind the counter with the condoms. The kit came with a miniature vial for collecting blood and a contraption for pricking your finger. I remember bringing the pre-addressed metered envelope containing my blood to the mailbox on the corner, wondering, how could this be accurate? Inside the kit was also a plastic card about the size of a credit card emblazoned with a phone number and a 15-digit code. I'd wait ten agonizing days to call a voice automated system and enter my 15-digit number, shaking, petrified, and a female automated voice would say, "Your HIV antibody test is... negative." I was always afraid I might hear, "Please hold for a customer service agent," which would mean I was positive. But I always got the automated voice.

I was negative, then.

I can only sense my soul when I'm looking down at my body.

I head out to go for a run, and as I am leaving my building, I see a package I have been waiting for inside the second door, leaning against a window. My Chinese herbs. I think about bringing it up to my apartment before my run, but that would mean I'd have to wash my hands, calm the dogs, so I tell myself, I'm only going out for a short run, I'll just bring it up when I get back, and in that moment I realize I am taking a chance, a risk the herbs will be stolen. When I get outside, I see the wind chime, I hear the wind chime, which makes me run faster, harder, longer, and it reminds me of when we used to take elevators—like someone who lets the elevator door close, even though they see you rushing to get in.

As the endorphins from my jog start to hit, I remember the Mexican soap opera I've been rewatching called *Cuando Llega el Amor.* It is one of those telenovelas that actually end, unlike the sprawling American type which go on for decades. The story revolves around two sisters. One is pretty and smart and nice and the other has a sort of strange look to her, she's a bitch. I like the bad sister. Both sisters ride horses and compete in racing competitions and they will soon be competing in the same contest and the bad sister really wants to win because the good sister has everything, a gorgeous fiancé and the love of all of her friends and family. So the bad sister is jealous, and with good reason, so she decides to put poison in the good sister's horse's food, but while the bad sister isn't looking the bad sister's horse eats the poisoned food, so, during the race, the bad sister's horse wipes out throwing the bad sister into a tree which turns her into a paraplegic for life while the good sister keeps winning the races and the bad sister is restrained to a wheelchair and all the while the good sister acts heroically, practically saves the bad sister's life and never leaves the bad sister's bedside.

Even though the bad sister is in a coma in the hospital, she can hear everyone raving about how great the good sister is, and this is making her crazy, making her hate the good sister even more, but she is unable to react. Finally, she wakes up, but refuses to talk. They move her home to the mansion where she is unable to leave her bedroom. A couple weeks later, there is a big party for the good sister, to celebrate her engagement with her beautiful fiancé, who the bad sister is in love with because he fucked her one night before the horse accident because the good sister wouldn't put out, and the bad sister faked a pregnancy which was soon found out to be a hoax. The party is one of those extravagant affairs that rich people give, in which there is a gazebo and tents and everyone raves about what a great person the good sister is, and such a good racer, and so beautiful, the kind of person that brings a smile to everyone's face, kind of like Mary Tyler Moore. So, she tells EVERYONE how MUCH she LOVES them and about how she just couldn't be HAPPIER. She is saying all of this stuff and the bad sister can hear all of it from her wheelchair, so, she electronically wheels herself to the balcony and starts screaming, *Te odio!!! Te odio!!!* in order to get everyone's attention, and then with her teeth she flings herself over the ledge, plunging to her death in front of God and everybody.

Do the guests at the party find this to be bad news, good news, or bad news that they are secretly happy about? Unbeknownst to everyone, the bad sister had planted a bomb in the wheelchair, so when the family rushes to the house, it blows up, killing everyone. Do the poor villagers in the neighborhood find this to be bad news or good news? What about the other society people? Are they secretly happy? We have to be careful. We don't want to give them what they want.

The bad sister shouldn't have been so careless with the poison.

My grandfather had one leg, ears the size of fists, and shocking red hair. He showed me how to open oysters with a screwdriver which I ate with Saltines and Tabasco. They slithered down my throat like lizards. He was a crabber, made most of his money off of soft-shell crabs. Their heads are poisonous so you have to cut them off before you cook them. My grandfather lost his leg in a train accident. He was working on top of a moving car when he fell off and was sucked under a train. His leg was neatly chopped off. He could see it on the other side of the track. He said he saw himself twice, once fully, connected to the leg, and the second time partial, two arms and a leg. I envied his wooden leg. I thought it better than the sacks of liquid which made up both of mine. He hid things in it. A bottle of Jack Daniel's, pills, a vial of mercury, guns.

I met a guy online who asked if he could photograph me. *A professional,* he said, *I work with implied narratives. You have a certain vacuous stare I really like in models.*
I agreed, not sure if I'd received a compliment. I'm used to a different kind of flattery: where I'm from, no one is this direct.
He took me to a part of town I did not know. Neon crosses hung from a gray chapel. Deserted. Tumbleweeds. A battered ace of clubs fluttered through the air.
The apartment for the shoot was squalid. I opened the freezer and found a big green plastic fly. Was it filled with water? Slime? There was a cat but he called it a dog. All I could think about was snuff porn and I got a hard-on.
He made me stand behind a door holding a cigar he stole from a fat man. I hate it when skinny people say *fat*. They should say *heavyset*.
I was relieved when he did not ask me to put it in my mouth.
In this shot, only my hand was visible and he said it looked suspicious.

Then he produced a gold plaster mold of the Virgin Mary with tears like sunflower seeds falling down her cheeks. Instinctively, I put my finger in her mouth and this guy went mad, snapping three rolls of film with only my hand in the frame. *It's so sexual.* The cat/dog wandered into one of the shots.

He pulled out a child's chair and asked me to pretend I was dead beside it. I did it. My eyes were closed so I couldn't tell whether or not he was getting my face. This gave me a hard-on. I rolled over, pressing my dick onto the hardwood floor.

I saw him the following week. He had the proofs in his backpack in a locker. All I could see was a series of small black squares, my hand here or my foot there, dismembered.

I read this essay called *The Tyranny of Structurelessness* by Jo Freeman about how when feminist consciousness-raising groups tried a non-hierarchical approach to organizing, an unspoken tyranny arose that was much worse than if they had just had some structure.

Two quotes from the essay:
"Contrary to what we would like to believe, there is no such thing as a structureless group."
"People would try to use the 'structureless' groups out of a blind belief that no other means could possibly be anything but oppressive."

And as a child, I wanted to be a slave, to be tied up. I once handcuffed myself to a desk at school and said, "Someone did this to me."

And I wanted to be split up.

A hundred eyes of night. More like a million, I thought. So—a rough time—spiraling—back to shooting up meth and sex where men beat the shit out of me, regularly, and I *knew* I had to get sober.

Let's see... ecstasy, GHB, special K, pot, Jack Daniel's, Xanax, meth.

I used to think I wasn't shooting up a lot but then when I ran out I'd go to the drawer and smoke the blood out of all the remaining needles and there were a lot of needles.

Someone organized an orgy in my apartment while I was coming in and out of consciousness—I don't remember anything but I *was* physically active during part of it.

And someone attending the orgy brought luggage with him, turned out this luggage was all of his belongings, so when the orgy was over, he had moved in.

He told me he was from Iran, but then I met someone later who said, "*He's just a regular guy from Michigan.*"

He carried a book in his bag, *History of America*.

And I only ever saw him eat an avocado and M&M's.

The day he moved in—my birthday—nobody from my real life remembered—but he knew—we sat on a bare mattress, stained, the orgy over, he took me in his arms while eating an M&M and his tooth fell out.

Later, when I realized he was reaching the limit of squatter's rights, I told him if he wanted to stay with me we both had to get sober. He pretended to love my dogs—like *don't kick me out I can't live without your dogs.*

So I left out some drugs I knew he couldn't resist and when he did them I asked him to move.

Which was kind of a dick move on my part.

But he wouldn't go, he wouldn't budge. He'd leave for orgies—he was also hooking—I don't know—but he left bags and bags of stuff, multiplying. When asked to leave, he'd cry.

And we all know a crying queen is a scheming queen.

I still didn't know his name, which seemed insane—that in this part of my life, I was dispatching with the triviality of names.

He went to a sex party and while there I called, "I'm getting in a car and bringing all your stuff—if you don't come meet me, I am going to leave your leather harnesses, webcams, and lube on the street."

We met at the Dunkin' Donuts on 8th Avenue and 24th Street, his home away from home—free Wi-Fi and a bathroom to shoot up in. I showed him his stuff in the trunk, gave him $200, and then paid the driver. He cried for the dogs, then I never heard from him again.

As soon as I was rid of him, I knew I loved him, wanted him back, we were meant to be together—God had brought us together—suddenly it all switched and I was besotted, forlorn, wanted to switch places with him—*Freaky Friday*—leave my body, go into his—the pain of detox—I'd experience it for him once and then again later for me—two detoxes.

But in the end, I could only fix myself, was sick a long time. Walking down 7th Avenue, six months later, I ran into him—pot belly, stumbling, carrying a foldable table lamp for reading, limp, drooping over like a dying plant. And around the bottom a brown plastic bag—yellow ties leaked off like liquid. He didn't recognize me.

And I remember the orgy where I wasn't the star even though it was in my apartment, *just give him too much so he'll pass out in the corner.*

For completism I wanted to walk up to him and ask his name. I saw him try to take a picture of the sunset, with a flash.

I imagine he lives somewhere in the Southwest where the crystal meth is cheap and the living's easy, a ranch, but he still has free internet—and is in one of those video chat rooms where people shoot up in unison—a quantum physics event—all over the world.

Or he's probably dead.

I wonder if when people kill themselves they don't leave as quickly, they circle around a bit.

It's funny when you feel as if you don't want anything more in your life except to sleep, or else to lie without moving. That's when you can hear time sliding past you, like water running.

I finish my run and as I return to my block the wind chime comes into view. I need a contraption that shoots out ectoplasm or slime to coagulate around the chime to silence it. Like in *Ghostbusters*. I see how the fire escape can be accessed, and I am tall, I think I could almost reach the ladder if I jumped, pulling it down, and see myself climbing, climbing up to the third floor, where I will rip out the chime, tossing it to the street, triumphant, but as I flash forward to this future, I see a spike on a fence below the fire escape, and I see myself falling, heading towards the spike, sphincter first, balancing for a moment on the bone of my carcass, then disemboweling. And if I somehow survive that, upon reaching the hospital, I would become infected with Covid—everyone is saying to avoid the hospital at all costs. I almost climb up half-wishing for this demise—it seems appropriate somehow. I survived the AIDS epidemic, survived crystal meth addiction, all to die by a fall in pursuit of a wind chime. This finish seems right, the last line of a poem that makes you read back up the page.

I'm not tempted by the relief of sentimentality.

I hate trigger warnings, but why didn't someone warn me about the wind chime?

And I don't know if it is because of the quarantine, but I am now retrieving old memories.

I seroconverted to HIV positive about 20 years ago. It was a big deal for three months—I was devastated—then I covered it with shame, blocked it away. I didn't tell anyone at the time and you know what Nietzsche said, *Shame is inventive.* I have no memories of my childhood, and I don't remember the five years after seroconverting, either. And I don't know if it is because of the new quietness of my neighborhood, and I don't know if it is because of the wind chime, and I don't know if it is because of this new pandemic, but I am remembering now.

I can only sense my soul when it is leaving my body.

When it happened, I had really thrown myself into self-destruction, and while I didn't catch it by having anal sex or shooting drugs, at that point I was only chipping and smoking—doing hot rails, which is, to the best of my memory, a way of inhaling crystal meth that involves coarse rocks and a gas stove. Having someone cum in your mouth after doing a hot rail—not a great idea.

I jumped in with no willing and eager friends around and when I sank, I sank to the sound of loud laughter.

And I'm taking my temperature every fifteen minutes. Everyone I know is taking their temperature every fifteen minutes.

I got a full body rash, was violently ill for months, could barely walk, went to Dr. Dave in the Lower East Side, then Callen-Lorde, and they did two tests—one test showing I was HIV negative, and also an early detection test indicating I was seroconverting in such a way that I would, with 99.9 percent certainty, eventually become positive. My recent mistakes felt so close, I wanted to reach into the past and undo them. If I could only undo them. I had a pre-existing ticket to go to Disney World with my sister and her family, and I took the final test right before my flight—I found out I was HIV positive at Disney World. Right after I got the call with the bad news, we went on an Aerosmith-themed ride, Rock 'n' Roller Coaster. Immediately after getting off the roller coaster I received a call from a scientific study where the guy conducting it dangled the possibility that if I took part, there was a small chance I could undo what had been done, undo the undoable. Because I knew I was seroconverting as I was seroconverting, I was a valuable test subject to them. He urged me to get on the first flight home.

At this point I saw myself sneak off to the graveyard.

I concocted a fake drama for my sister (I didn't dare tell her—the shame, the shame of how did I let this happen) and took the next flight back to NYC. As it turns out, I was in the control group, did not receive the experimental drug, but rather an outdated grouping of HIV drugs: Kaletra, AZT, and a third drug that is currently being touted as a potential remedy to Covid. These toxic drugs made me very sick—I was already so weak from the seroconversion, also, struggling to stay sober. I wanted to stop taking these drugs. I asked to exit the study, but they pleaded with me to stay, brought me in to meet the lead researcher, and he spent a long time telling me how important my participation was for their numbers, that a lot of money had already been spent on my data. He seemed so handsome and rich, and I felt so wretched. My clothes tattered, my skin sallow. They kept saying I was in such a rare position to give back to my community, and in my own estimation I had been so bad, so irresponsible to contract this disease, that I did stay in the study, out of shame and out of guilt. I realized later that I'd also stayed because of a misplaced loyalty to them, as whatever sham cure they were touting had failed. In fact, some of the subjects in the test group even died. His promise of a potential remission turned out to be a lie. They just needed subjects for their experiment, and were willing to do anything to get them. And this makes me wonder, will I be first in line for the Covid vaccine?

Am I a monster or is this what it means to be a person?
I finally got a real doctor and he was alarmed by the study, insisted I go off of it immediately. I became obsessed with nefarious scientific studies of the past where test subjects were exploited. Lobotomies, teeth extractions, electroconvulsive therapy.

I began to have this recurring dream:
Everyone I knew was
being replaced by robotic
versions of themselves.
I was taken into a futuristic train by an ad man
real slick
from the sixties,
tie, metallic suitcase, martini,
and I was drugged-up,
an assembly line of drugged-up people.
The ad man at the front
sucking life force out with a futuristic vacuum
type suck thing up to the head
BAM
out comes your essence
(and everything else).
A factory for lobotomies.
Then he'd pluck out the eyeballs
with his fingers and put them in a jar.
Only the drugs
didn't work on me,
a very high threshold
so I started to come out of it a little bit,

like someone for whom anesthetic
doesn't work,
the movie where the patient can't
respond but is awake for an appendectomy
or an unnecessary amputation.
I snap out of it a little more
and wander in a different direction
away from the line
(I didn't want to be replaced by a robot)
like a zombie, cogent but barely.

But I have always wanted a lobotomy. Or electroconvulsive therapy. I hear afterwards, you feel a little high, a freelapse. I've never been able to convince anyone to give me either, but I heard if you have enough money there is a guy who will come to your house and give you both.

After going off the meds from the study my numbers got weird quickly. My doctor said in the old days I would have died within months, died first, and honestly some part of me wanted to reject the medication—*just let me die out*. I felt I didn't deserve help. I'm not sure why, but this idea that I would have died quickly made me feel so guilty.

I did go on other meds right away. At that time doctors liked to wait as long as possible before starting medication, but I couldn't wait. I don't know if it was because of the study that my disease progressed so quickly. I guess it doesn't matter—the new meds worked. My testosterone levels plummeted because of the HIV infection, and I am required to get a testosterone shot every two weeks. After each shot, my life becomes strange for about 48 hours.

Every thought is tied to heavy weights.

Although they weren't half as bad as AZT, the new drugs were also toxic. I went to an acupuncturist for the nausea, fatigue, confusion, nightmares. She gave me Chinese herbs. The pills really helped—they are called Six Gentlemen—six pills a day, three after lunch, three after dinner.

And I've taken them religiously since then, up until this current pandemic, when suddenly, maybe because of China, they are impossible to get. But my acupuncturist found some, and had them drop-shipped to my building on Ludlow Street between Houston and Stanton.

This is the package I've left in my lobby, for my run.

I somehow get past the wind chime, and when I return to my building, the package is gone, has been stolen I assume, and something snaps, I scream a trail of obscenities. With my gloved hand I rip the tops off all the garbage cans in my lobby, then punch the wall with both fists as hard as I can. Later, a bruise. I go to the front of the building, forgetting to be careful with the door knobs, and lean into the full row of buzzers.

Immediately, everyone is trying to buzz me in, without even asking who I am. I see the wind chime in the distance. It makes me want to tear the entire block down. I run up the stairs and two of my neighbors poke their heads out—I put my mask on, and we stay six feet apart, and I say, "My package is missing, my Chinese herbs, which will be good for nobody but me, have been stolen," The athletic straight neighbor, Thaddeus, tells me, "There was a guy rustling outside my door. He was going through packages, told me he was cold. A white guy with a red face. I gave him an orange jacket because he told me he was cold."

And while I think it is very sweet of Thaddeus to give this guy a jacket, I want to ask him why he let him walk out with my package, but I don't. For some reason I think: *Please God, forgive me for feeling anxiety and guilt when other people have bigger problems.*

I say, "I'm going to go look for him." It feels like every word I say has chains around its ankles and as I storm out the door, again forgetting all my protocols, I hit the sidewalk, and I am confronted with the wind chime. The urge to throw something at it is immense and I remember what it feels like to have a dealer toy with me, make me socialize with him when all I want is my drugs.

I touch my nose again with my bare hand that had been on the door knob. At this point I feel like an old-school bug chaser, so the day counting starts again. I'm hearing *you are safe after 11 days.*

I remember reading somewhere that we only begin to live when we conceive of life as a tragedy and then I suddenly feel good—does that mean I am manic? Am I worthy of this destruction? Am I sturdy enough?

Dreams have a short life in the memory.

Memories have a short life in the memory.

And I don't know if it is because of the quarantine, the quiet, but as I head out to look for the guy with a red face in the orange jacket, I have a new memory:

I guess you could say I was sexually precocious. I discovered my parents' vibrator when I was eight. It was of the old-fashioned type. Gray and heavy with tight long springs for handles, that later, when I grew them, would snag my pubes. It was like my brain was exploding. I used it so much my legs were sore and it was hard to walk for days at a time. The vibrator used so much electricity that when plugged in, it made all of the televisions in the house go fuzzy. So, when any of the family members were using the vibrator, everyone else in the house knew it was being used, because, in my house, the television was always on, and there was a television in every room. A strange unspoken scrutiny, a shared shame.

My parents had a copy of *The Joy of Sex*, which they hid, not very well, under my father's bed. Some pages were folded in, so I knew the type of sex my parents liked best. The print on the hand-job page was all worn down.

I remember looking for something to stick my penis in when I was a child. I found a toothbrush holder in the bathroom that seemed to be the correct size, in the shape of an aqua-blue fish, its mouth open wide. Once I stuck my dick in the fish's mouth, it grew far too large to come back out. I knew I shouldn't have done what I did, but I couldn't keep from trying it. I passed out, my head banged on the toilet. During my blackout I had a dream I was aboard a hijacked plane. The hijackers tied me up and measured my penis. Mine was too small. The hijacker said I had malgrowth and would never get hair under my arms or opaque semen or a large penis because I had masturbated so much, and with a vibrator, even worse. Another hijacker in a ski mask and an orange jacket came up to me. He pressed his finger into my anus and said, "I like 'em tight." It was at this point that I came in the fish.

When I regained consciousness, I was staring up from beside the toilet, my mother pounding on the door telling me she didn't know how many times she had asked me not to lock the bathroom door. The fish was still gripping my penis. I looked to the toilet as if it could give me advice. I was hoping somewhere down there in the plumbing a muted voice might emerge telling me what to do next.

My father banged down the door. My mother put her hands to her nose. We had to crack open the fish with a hammer as if it were a piggy bank. Semen spilled into the sink and everyone got to see the size of my penis. I said with all earnestness that it was an accident. That it just sort of fell in.

Then, in my mid-twenties, when I lived in England, I had a job recording phone sex announcements. My specialty was a southern hick in a barn: hard-on, overalls, lots of hay, incest. I got paid in cash, 90 pounds for an hour, not bad for just talking. Besides, it was creative. I was using my brain making up stories. One time, on the way back to the Tube, my wallet was stolen, all my IDs, credit cards, money. I walked thirty blocks to the LION, a bar that specialized in older men buying younger men drinks. I went home with a strange man who didn't know Madonna was American. He said he was brain damaged. He gave me three mysterious pills and some acid. He said it was only coincidence he lived in a home for the mentally challenged. A social worker walked in while we were lying on the bed, just as my acid started to kick in. I laughed, couldn't form a sentence. I figured the social worker thought I must also be brain damaged.

I started to hallucinate chicken carcasses falling from the ceiling and a strange metal grid filling the room, holding up flaps of rotting flesh, all in those psychedelic colors. The social worker left and the guy tried to hump me. I was so freaked out I pretended to sleep, but he didn't stop. He started to eat the flesh off my feet. I stumbled up, threw on half of my clothes. He blocked the way so I couldn't leave, he was bulky, strong, and not tripping. I begged—*let me go.* Finally, he let me by. At this point we were both crying. He screamed down the stairwell, "I can't believe you're leaving me like this." I was in a strange part of London. I had no idea where I was, no wallet, no money. I was tripping, waiting for the peak to pass. For five hours I wandered the streets. I got home to find policemen waiting for me in my stairwell. They had found my wallet—no money—under a mattress in the apartment of someone shady who'd been caught in a VCR and camcorder heist. Did I know them? Could they come in and ask me some questions? I ran to the bathroom, flushed my stash down the toilet and made them some tea. I wanted to turn on the TV for a dose of reality, but before I sat down the telephone rang. It was my pimp, the one from my new escort service. He had a punter into policemen, could I pick up a uniform?

So, there was this guy with a steel cage in his basement—he wanted me to wear a police uniform, knock me out, a total KO scene. Like where the submissive takes Ativan, but he found out I was sober and couldn't, so he wanted me to be his slave. At first I thought—hot—until he said: "My roommate has this silly idea of paying a maid to clean our apartment."

Suddenly the idea didn't seem so hot.

He said he also liked the idea of abusing a cop—to degrade a *nice* cop with integrity—this I could get excited about.

I went to a special cop store to buy the uniform: a badge, aviator glasses, and a plastic nightstick from a leather store on Old Compton Street (it had to be plastic because if you were going to stick it in, you'd have to be able to clean it). I rode my bike to his place, in Brixton. When I'd enter I'd give him a citation, we would fight, fuck, then I'd bike home.

So, I was ready. When he answered the door, I was ready with a scene and dialogue—but instead, we were not alone, his roommate was at the kitchen table making pie crust. I hid the nightstick—suddenly—a gay sitcom. These guys had money.

He told me to take off my shoes so as not to dirty the apartment. And the roommate, before looking at me, turned to the guy (whose name I still didn't know), and said:

"Tell *it* to go get the brown sugar."

Against my better judgment, I went to get the brown sugar. Or I should say, "*It* went."

I looked in three different corner shops before I found any.

I felt like Carrie, all dressed up in a prom dress, tiara, cop gear I had spent hundreds of dollars on (going to a prom would have cost less). And the brown sugar—pig's blood.

Hence my therapist's point that I masochistically seduce the aggressor in the world around me, until, no matter how hard the world tries to make things turn out otherwise, I end up being Carrie. And by the way, looking like a cop in this neighborhood felt strange—I desperately wanted to explain to the shopkeepers that I wasn't a cop... but...
When I got back, dinner was served and there was an expectation that I would sit at a different table and wait on them while they ate.
I ignored this and sat with them—my one act of rebellion.
I wish I had sat at the little slave table.
The salad had alfalfa sprouts on it and they started talking about musical theater.
And I thought—WHAT IS THE SAFE WORD.

And I still didn't know his first name, and at that point I didn't care. What had been hot about this was the steel cage he kept in the basement, and he had told me he knew someone in Birmingham who wanted to be killed.

He didn't use the word *kill*—just that the guy wanted to be taken out altogether, to end it for good, and this guy discussing musical theater, he wanted to help him do it.

They started talking about *Wicked*, and the meanings of the songs therein. Any other musical would have been… better.

And I was thinking, is this a kind of new-fangled perverse sadism? A scene they'd devised to bring the torture to a new high. (singing) *Popular, I want to be popular.* THERE WERE NO SAFE WORDS THERE.

I stayed.

And dinner was over, and the roommate started clapping and singing a cleanup song:

(clapping and singing)

Clean up clean up clean up—and now we clean it up! Clean up clean up clean up!

And I realized this song was meant as a prompt for me to clear the table for them.

And I thought *what film is this.*

Chinese Roulette?

And, like the brown sugar, for some invisible reason, I cleared the table as if moved by my own remote control.

Am I a monster? Or is this what it means to be a person?
I'm not sure why I submitted—maybe to see how far I could take it—how Carrie could I get, how far could I push that line? None of this was in my erotic lexicon but I was interested.

Eventually—his bedroom. He rifled through my bag when I wasn't looking and retrieved my nightstick. I let him beat me with it, but he didn't really.

He put me in a strangle hold and as he choked me out he whispered into my ear, "Say Good Night Faggot."

And I said, "Good Night Faggot."

A vain repetition—that's what it was, a vain repetition.

...that sounds like something an addict would say.

...this is what it takes...

There was no particular feeling around this. No fairy-tale degradation, or dark night of the soul.

Just brown sugar, pie crust.

You are a victim. There's no endurance in your face. Victims are necessary so that the strong may exercise their will.

And I don't believe alcoholism is a disease any more than depression is.

As I am coming out of this memory, I find myself storming across Rivington Street. By now it is bitter and gloomy outside, and everything has gone out of me except for a persistent feeling of guilt. My neighbor, the photographer, said I should check the garbage cans, maybe he will just throw them away, so I turn my phone into a flashlight and peer into each can. Our neighborhood has never been cleaner because everyone has left. For the first time I can remember, the cans aren't overflowing, and it is easy to look through the garbage. I have never done this before, and I think, *look at all the new experiences the pandemic is affording me*. I head towards Roosevelt Park—if anywhere, he'll be there. As I cross Eldridge Street looking for the guy in the orange jacket with a red face, I remember my dealer who used to live on this block. He walked with one of those propulsive gaits you see with some meth-addicted people—they call it "gross movements" as with Parkinson's disease. And I remember the time he was hospitalized because he got blood poisoning from shooting up. He told me they thought he almost died, or did die, for a little while. Even though I was sober during that time, I brought him a new phone to the hospital, because I knew somewhere deep down inside, I wasn't done with drugs yet, and that later, he'd give me more.

When I get to Roosevelt Park I look for my guy. I am stunned by the level of desperation I encounter. I no longer care about my herbs or even the wind chime. An orange jacket moves quickly out of the shadows and I think I feel a dull thud on the back of my skull, edges start to grey, and as I pass out and feel myself hitting the pavement, it's as if the force has opened neural networks, retrieving memory function.

When I was little, my biggest fantasy was to join a cult. Everyone said they were so bad, but the people in them seemed so happy. The Hare Krishnas I sometimes saw downtown—yes we even had Hare Krishnas in the south—seemed happy, and sexy. I mean they were hot, all those shaved heads and baggy clothes. The cult members depicted in my Catholic school religion book always smiled more than my parents, more than the nuns, even more than the girls in the fucking folk guitar group in church. So I thought, *I'd like to be in a cult.*

I hated my body, was a chubby kid. I thought I was fat, so I wanted the costume of the baggy clothes to cover everything. I hated my wiry uncontrollable hair, dry and frizzy, so the shaved head, I wanted that. And the dots. I wanted those dots.

I saw a documentary about Charles Manson on public television. I didn't understand what was going on, but I thought Manson, Manson and all those girls, they were great. I wanted to be a part of it.

I had a lot of sexual energy as a child.

We'd go on family trips driving from North Carolina to Mississippi, my father driving, my mother, the passenger, and me sprawled across the back seat. My father would smoke Winstons blowing the cigarette smoke through a crack in the window. I would listen to Janis Joplin on my Walkman, and play with myself underneath a Snoopy and Woodstock-themed beach blanket, while my mother passed plastic cups filled with cool water from a green beat-up plastic thermos with a white cap. When it got late, we'd stop at a cheap motel where the other guests were truckers, roaches in the tub. Thin scratchy blankets.

We checked in and I went to get ice. I found the public motel bathroom, drew a picture of a penis and a pair of big lips on the bathroom stall wall, the date—I'd be back at 2 AM, *anybody want a blow job?* It was hot, the fantasy, the smell, the stains on the wall, other drawings and invitations for sex, a phone number scrawled. I wanted to call the number, but didn't know how. It was intoxicating. The writings on the walls felt like promises.

I went back to the hotel room and tried to sleep—two strangely square beds only a foot apart. I looked to the clock: 1 AM, another hour to wait. I was a prostitute, ready to be ravaged, wanting to do it for free for the truckers. A gift, giving back, my offering would save me. I stared up at the water stains on the drop ceiling, patterns. A spiderweb, then a spider. The TV flickered, a black-and-white movie, a woman from the thirties talked and talked, her mouth moved like a joke shop set of disembodied teeth that clack and clack and clack until they fall off the table. My father woke up, got on top of my mother, humped her, dazed. Only half awake, she said, *not now*, but he kept humping and humping and she rolled away, him, mad. I was titillated, repulsed. While he pseudo-forced my mother to have sex I closed my eyes and fantasized about being downstairs in the grimy bathroom, on my knees, blindfolded, waiting, a fat boy waiting to take all comers.

And then it shifted—some part of me wanted to be my mother.

She didn't get him off. He got out of bed and I heard him jerk off into the toilet.

I was thinking, I'd have gotten him off.

The next day we pulled into a Stuckey's, an interstate roadside store where they sell gas, lunch, and wooden marble mazes. I went in to buy taffy, flat, long, yellow, tasting like fake banana, wrapped in thin wax paper. On my way out I saw people in maroon robes getting into a van. They had shaved heads, rosy cheeks. And they had the dots, big big smiles, a guitar.

I knew how to play guitar. I was in the folk guitar group at church. I could strum. *Down down up up down up down down up up down up.* One of them picked up the guitar and started to play. My mother was in the bathroom filling the green thermos.

My father had finished gassing up the car, and walked away to smoke. Escape called for me. I saw myself, as in a dream, grab the yellow taffy, one strip in each hand, small barbells for fat people, and I ran for my life. I saw myself dive into the van just as the doors were closing, like a movie, like the six-million-dollar woman, falling on my back, people sitting on orange puffy cushions, staring at me.

"Drive!" I yelled. "Drive!"

In my fantasy, they did drive. They obeyed *me.*

When I regain consciousness I'm lying on the sidewalk, looking up at a streetlight and I swear I can hear the wind chime, though that is impossible, it is five blocks away. A police car glides onto the sidewalk and before I can sit up two policemen are bent over me.

And I hear myself saying, "Orange Jacket. Orange Cushions." One of them shakes me, and it bothers me he is touching me. And again I hear myself speaking, "I'm sure you have bigger fish to fry but I had a package stolen. I think I was attacked, I don't know what to do."

They ask me if I want to make a report. I say, "Aren't you sort of busy right now?" I feel guilty for taking their time. I don't want to bother them, or create work for them.

I worry, if I make a report will he be arrested and brought into a prison where he will die of Covid? They are treating me with kid gloves, like they are worried about my mental health, and when they investigate the back of my head, they say they can't see anything.

They ask to meet me back at my apartment because I don't have my driver's license with me. I purposefully hadn't brought my wallet to the park. Are they going to take me in for a psych eval? I head back to my building anyhow.

I go upstairs to get my license, wash my hands, and before I am done, they ring my buzzer, waiting for me downstairs. They take the report, and I am so stressed out I have a hard time stringing together the few details of the story. I can't even say with any certainty that I was hit. They touch my license, which scares me, and then one of the cops keeps moving his face mask to his chin and I can't understand why he is doing that. Because he can?

I ask them if they can hear the wind chime. They cannot. I want to ask them if there is anything they could do about the wind chime but I stop myself and remember that age old adage—*don't always tell your psychiatrist the truth.*

They give me a case number and a phone number and I go upstairs to my apartment to disinfect my license. I swab my nostrils with Listerine.

Ten minutes later someone knocks at my door, it is Thaddeus, the straight neighbor, without a mask, asking me if he can buy a little whisky, that he feels like drinking. I tell him I don't drink, that I don't have any alcohol, and slam the door in his face. I can't understand why he would come to my door without a mask. Immediately after the door closes I feel guilty—the last thing I need right now is another enemy in the building. I sit at my computer, and then remember, I do have some Everclear, 190 proof, that I've been using to sterilize my phone. I put on my mask, go to Thaddeus' apartment, and before I even knock on the door, he has opened it.

"I forgot I had this Everclear that I've been using to sterilize things, it's really strong, 190 proof, you should be really careful, but do you want some?"

He half closes his door and puts a handkerchief around his face. I am grateful for this. He holds out a grubby tin cup and I half fill it. Again, I say, "Be careful, it is very strong."

"Don't worry, I'm not really a drinker," he says, and as I turn to leave he stops me, indicating he would like a little more, so I pour another inch.

And I think, isn't that the way it is…
I don't want him feeling like he doesn't have enough.
But I worry about sharing my stash. It is impossible to find alcohol of any kind above 60 proof in the Lower East Side. And this worry about my stash makes me wonder, *will I drink the Everclear? Am I building up to a relapse?*

When I get back to my apartment, I look at the back of my head with my cell phone camera.

It is clear no one has hit me. I don't know why I passed out. I am embarrassed. I remember the time I tried to sue my landlord because of a house fire I thought was his fault and upon investigation by the fire department they found a candle for cooking up I had clearly left burning when I went out to cop more. As a sober alcoholic, I feel really strange about having just poured my neighbor a drink. I call my photographer friend who lives next door, and explain to her that I am worried the guy with the orange jacket and the red face will get brought in and contract Covid and die in jail and it will all be my fault. She tells me the cops won't do anything—there is no real description, no surveillance camera footage, no proof. I call my sponsor to tell on myself. *Do I owe an amend?* I leave a message for my therapist.

My current therapist is the very first one I haven't written long, single-spaced desperate explanatory letters to, nor urgent emotional emails. I would write a thousand-word email to Dr. Cohen trying to tell her what I was realizing about what she needed to do to help me or just desperate thoughts, and it was so humiliating to get these caring one-sentence responses, "Sent from my iPhone."

This monologue is like an anti-Facebook post where you post all the shameful details about yourself.

A little later I am freaked out about the letter my old therapist sent to my insurance company where she said she had changed her diagnosis to narcissistic personality disorder.

And then the other therapist who basically said my problem is that I am a bitch.

And then the next therapist who wrote a letter and sent it to me and said he had changed his diagnosis of me to borderline personality disorder and he said, "We could prescribe medication but it won't really help. You will spend the rest of your life in and out of mental institutions."

That didn't bother me because he had a book on his desk with puffy letters, a bestseller clearly bought at the checkout line in the grocery store. And he had very wide ties when it wasn't fashionable.

And then that other therapist who said of me: grandiosity, lack of empathy, difficult to work with, incurable due to a lack of insight. Diagnosis: basically a total asshole with no redeeming qualities et cetera.

My current therapist eventually calls me back and he points out that even if I wasn't hit, it was very dangerous to go to the park because I was clearly looking for a fight and maybe the guy in the orange jacket was, too. His only other comment is that he thinks Thaddeus was trying to hit on me, but I don't agree. I picture myself with a sign above my head, "WHORE," and I wonder what this comment from my therapist says about my therapist—it seems odd.

A memory. Before I enter their apartment I had already taken three hits of speed and two shots of whisky. I was immediately blindfolded. A flash of light and the cameras were rolling. He was Middle Eastern, short, muscular. Before it went dark I saw a young man bent over his knees—someone had written words all over his body. Blood was coming out of his ass. They gave me some pills to take but I thought they were just Advil because I didn't feel anything but I pretended to pass out anyhow. An instructional video on how to beat ass. At the edge of my vision I saw he was wearing a fanny pack. He kept wrapping the whip around my ass to the side, where it hurt too much. They peed in a glass and told me to drink it but I said *I only drink from the tap.* One of the guys was freaked out by me and left. The other started to fuck me and strike me across the face. I said *hit me harder hit me harder* and he did. I told him I loved him, and to hit me harder. He stopped, told me to leave.

I'd won again.

It must seem like I was marveling at my own self-degradation, or spiraling down, but really, I was in power, when I let men do these things to me I was in control. What they did to me became them. I transformed them into demons.

ToeTag loved me. His screen name referred to the tags you find tied to the toes of corpses. I loved ToeTag back. We never spoke because when he came over I was dead.

He had given me directions on how to pose within a specific stage of rigor mortis. Mouth open, not wide. Arms by my side. Legs straight out. Limbs heavy. He picked them up. I let them drop. He rolled me over—I plopped down. He invited people over to fuck me in the ass. He came in my mouth once. He brought over embalmer tools. He told me he loved me. He also had zip ties—the plastic industrial type—he tied me to things. In life I think he was a real estate broker, married. One time, the best time, he wrapped me in plastic and left me to suffocate. But he came back and ripped the plastic before I could die. We never spoke. I was dead when he came over and dead when he left. After, he wrote me e-mails telling me I should keep a cleaner house. He paid for my pedicures.

I force myself to eat something, and get in bed with my dogs, try to calm myself. I have a large orange vase and when I look at it, I remember the orange cushions, the orange jacket. I try to meditate and focus on my breath, but I can hear the wind chime wafting in from my cracked window. I blame the wind chime for all of this. I close the window, but I can still hear the wind chime. Even though it is cold out, I turn on my air conditioner to try to block it out, but I can still hear it, tinkling. I turn on the TV, the blender, the microwave, the tea pot, the vacuum. I even open the spigots. I can still hear the wind chime.
And amid this cacophony I finally begin to drift towards sleep,
I'm remembering still…

How my upstairs neighbors, the ones with a baby, had left a carriage in the lobby AGAIN. It was old, a pram, huge and completely inappropriate for the city. I imagine they had chosen it for aesthetic reasons. This couple was going for a certain baby carriage retro look (which somehow made me hate them even more). I became enraged.

They thought they could leave their personal property in a shared space just because they had offspring. We had to step around their garbage, our maintenance person had to work around their baby carriage. Without breaking a sweat, or thinking, I grabbed the pram and rolled it onto the sidewalk, right onto Ludlow between Houston and Stanton, calmly entered my apartment, made something to eat, ate it, went to sleep, mentioned none of this to anybody. Like one of those murders where someone stabs their cheating husband and then watches a movie, boils an egg as if nothing had happened. Psychopathic. Like that.

The next day I overslept, a rage hangover, but as I left my apartment I noticed a sign taped to the dirty wall asking for information about the "stolen" carriage, asking it be returned, soliciting information, a picture of the baby carriage on the sign, haunted, like something from *It's Alive*, or *Rosemary's Baby*.

As soon as I saw the sign I felt terrible—as if I had been in a slumber—as if someone other than me had disposed of the carriage, like *please don't let the dead body in the other room be at my doing.* I wondered, did this mean I was on the verge of a relapse? I called my sponsor, then a friend, and no one knew quite what to say but my next-door neighbor looked deeply into my eyes with a kind of faux empathy, "*Are you OK*?" and this made me feel wretched, like her worry made me a worse person than I actually was, this doubt of my sanity became my personality. Eventually, my sponsor said that what I did was basically akin to stealing, she affected a deep concern for my psychic well-being, and I became terrified I would have to make a formal apology, and if I didn't, I would drink, if I didn't publicly apologize the next thing you know, a needle in my arm, and would they call the police once they found out it was me who took it? I didn't have the money to replace the baby carriage… *Maybe leave a gift certificate to BUY BUY BABY taped to the sign? But how much does an antique baby carriage cost?*

I could put up my own sign offering babysitting services
Or or
Stalk them
Or
Befriend them and find out who they think did it. Lean into it, spend time with them just to heighten anxiety and guilt. And I could see this turning into a horror movie where the children end up in a trash bin.

But the truth is I worried about myself—was I setting myself up to get fucked up in the most fucked-up way possible (like smoking crack). Once I start I never stop. Years, and I mean years of selling my soul for what? A baby carriage?

You'd put in your money and guide the claw—an alien hand with three slender fingers—over a mountain of stuffed animals modeled on famous creatures from Hollywood movies, it drops, and you hope it snags something. This time, it pulled up a brown paper bag with grease spots on it, as if something gross was inside.

The claw carried the bag over to a chute and dropped it, at which point it fell into a basket on the outside of the contraption. I understood somehow that there was a baby in the bag, not a bomb or anything like that, but a baby and that there was something wrong with it. The air he breathed in he couldn't breathe out; and I saw the baby swell up and swell up till his body and face were grotesquely deformed; as if he were about to split into three versions of himself and for a second I thought he might explode. Both I and the parents were horrified, in anguish, but I was especially anxious because I knew that in order to save him I would have to puncture the baby with a huge pin, so he could split. The mother was the only one who took action.

She went over to the baby and started to strip off its skin as if she were peeling an orange. It was no good. The baby kept swelling, especially his head and belly.

I never dream of the police.

Instead, I dream a lot about doctors, babies, and x-rays.

Or that I was in love with a man, and as we were having
sex, he kept getting
younger and younger
so that by the end of it he was a
baby, and we were still having sex
until we were done
at which point I put him
in the
antique pram and I was
I was
a…a… a… a pedophile.
And I tried to explain
when the sex
started, he was a grown man
but they looked to the baby
carriage, and back to me,
the sun was shining
no blackouts
nowhere to hide
everyone can see I had sex with
not even a child but a baby
and the shame I experience in that moment is
complete

But I adjusted his
little baby hat
anyway
to keep the sun
from his eyes.

And then I was on that futuristic train again, with the ad man, and it was going over a bridge.
Suddenly the bridge was gone, and we were crashing straight towards the ground.

I die in dreams all the time.

I try to put together the chain of events from the night before, the herbs, Thaddeus, the orange jacket, the park, but everything feels disjointed. My brain is full of concrete but I have three instant coffees and go on the internet to google people I resent. This is a barometer of how bad my spiritual condition is. My dogs Marlena and Whitey fight. I check how many views on a YouTube video of a reading series I helped with. Not very many. So I do a gratitude list:

I am grateful I feel fat today.
I am grateful I know when to be the bigger person.
I am grateful for societal collapse.
I am grateful to be sober.
I am grateful I have the opportunity to meditate today.
I am grateful for exercise addiction.
I am grateful I will never have a group of friends like regular people.
I am grateful I am the kind of person you don't want at your wedding.
I am grateful I am staying in NYC for the pandemic.
I am grateful I have food in the freezer.
I am grateful I am not sick.
I am grateful I feel trapped and can't get away.

This gratitude list doesn't work because I open my computer again and go online.
The New York Times likes things I hate. I feel out of step with the world. If I had a magic wand I would be a morning person. I would be thin. I would be a person who naturally recycles. Why do I care about theater and art when I am barely a part of it, a fringe figure at best, no social media presence, a ghost.
In a way, I'm glad it has all been stopped. All those voices shouting at me for attention.

Good night.

Someone gave me a television. She couldn't stand me not having one. It was really small, you could put it in the closet. A Mega Watchman. I plugged it in. Changed the channels. The sadness set in quickly. Suddenly I was twelve years old, at home, sitting at the kitchen table, trying to swallow okra whole, the TV on loud, then louder—my father really wanted to see this part.

I unplugged the television and stared at it. I could see my reflection. I looked too old. I put it away. I thought about giving it to poorer people. They shouldn't have one either. A friend called. A famous diver with AIDS was on the Barbara Walter show. I decided to turn on the television which I could not find. I remembered it was in the closet. The diver was still endorsed by Speedo even though he had AIDS. He was depressed. They kept showing the clip where he hit his head on the board and there was blood in the water. Barbara was worried. Later, one of the Judds had a commercial on viral hepatitis. She had a number to call for information. I wished I had seen that before I moved to Mexico and caught it myself.

I turned it off and tried to go to sleep. I was restless and wanted to turn it on again. I entered a dream where I was a maid cleaning up a ritzy apartment. The owner had a television in every room. All of the televisions were always on. I cut my knee on a piece of glass and bled onto the white carpet. I reached for my green sponge and the bottle of soft scrub, frantically rubbing, trying to get the stain out. I was badly hurt, I continued to bleed, but I didn't seem to care. When I woke, I was sleepwalking, biting into a sponge like a bone.

It's four months later, and the neighborhood is loud again, the outdoor dining feels like a carnival. Sometimes I think it has never been louder. I can barely hear the wind chime, but when I walk by, I look up at it, and think about meeting its owners, and inviting them to hear me.

But on this Monday morning, there are no trucks on the street, and the restaurants aren't open, and it is windy, and I can hear the wind chime, but it sounds muted. I take the dogs out for a walk, and I look up at it, and it is a little tangled, as if it has hanged itself.

I fight the urge to climb up and untangle the strings to free it. I'm happy to hear the wind chime, even muted, because I haven't been remembering things, but now I do.

After I extracted myself from Scientology, which was rough—it's almost easier to just go along with the plan so they will in essence leave you alone—I felt I needed something else, and this new workspace I was renting had a room where you could meditate or take power naps. The idea was people who engage in Buddhist meditation are more productive, so I started going to the room to meditate, and I met a woman who invited me to the Shambhala Institute on 22nd Street just west of 6th Avenue near where the Barnes & Noble used to be. I don't think the Shambhala Institute is there anymore either—a #MeToo scandal forced it to close.

God, forgive me for thinking and feeling other people's feelings, actions, choices, wants, needs, well-being, lack of well-being and ultimate destiny.

I have had lovers the way a Buddhist has friends, hundreds of them, all meaning the same. I loved them as all humankind, as a socket accepts prongs, a good time, sympathy fucks, messy mantras—just an acknowledgment of our impermanence, our wasting, and, like a Buddhist, when one of them died, I did not mourn him like a parent or a wife, I mourned more for everything disintegrating. This new kind of Buddhism is not like '80s Buddhism in which businessmen travel with shrines in briefcases and yell at their secretaries, flirt with temps. No, not that, it's downwardly mobile, more like a prostitute deciding not to charge.

I went to an orientation session at the Shambhala Institute, and decided to do the Level One training which is a weekend of meditation and lectures. I spent many hours, sitting, open-eyed meditation, and I was encouraged to gently rest my gaze six feet in front of me and focus on my breathing. For the entire weekend I was sat in the front row. And six feet in front of me, where I focused my gaze for hours and hours, was a radiator, and underneath, a red and yellow box of rat poison. It actually had a skull and crossbones on the side of the box, and a warning, and this was burned into my retinas from staring at it for 15 hours, "DO NOT INGEST. CAN INDUCE COMAS IN HUMANS." The longer I sat there the more upset I became about the plight of the rats. I thought about PETA and where are they when it comes to rats, and I became enraged that in the same room of peace and Tonglen meditation, and absorbing the pain of the world, there would also be a fucking box of rat poison! I mean isn't it the Buddha who went out of his way to rescue a fly? Couldn't they at least *hide* the *poison*. So, Monday morning I decided to file a complaint. I called the Shambhala Institute and explained to them where I was sat, and how I was forced to stare at a box of rat poison for 15 hours. I told the lady that I thought they should get a "Have a Heart" trap. I heard her snicker.

As if she didn't even consider a rat an animal. She put me on hold. After a few minutes, a guy picked up the line. He apologized and said he would immediately remove the poison, that I was right, that it shouldn't be there. I felt better.

I went back a couple of weeks later for a regular sitting meditation, but really I wanted to check up on the rat poison. To make sure it was gone, to make sure my complaint was heard. But it still sat there, under the radiator. "DO NOT INGEST. CAN INDUCE COMAS IN HUMANS." Without hesitating and in front of the monk and all the students, I walked right up to the radiator, crossing the sacred space without bowing to the statue of some deity, picked up the rat poison, and left, again without bowing. Nobody's head moved, nobody made a sound, but their eyes were darting around in their sockets so much I swear I could hear a squishy sound, like mastication, or it looked like they were all blind, with their eyes open not seeing. And in that moment I was struck with this idea that we are just bags of skin, roaming around from point A to point B, filled with decomposing food. I was so flustered upon leaving that I walked through the backstage area of the (I guess) temple and it was odd to see things they used for the rituals lined up on the wall like stage props. And there was one prop, a series of cylinders for ringing, like a wind chime.

I can hear the wind chime and I have a memory of being in a similar area in a Catholic church when I was 12, the Sacristy.
It was time for my first communion but I was terrified of the eucharistic host. I refused to participate out of fear so the priest brought me backstage to show me the host was kept in a big plastic garbage bag with a scoop like an ice machine at a motel.
I had always thought they kept the host in drawers like insects in the science museum pinned down in rows and rows of thin drawers.
My mother was disturbed by my fear of the body of Christ, like I was Damien Omen, checking my scalp for the number of the beast. One time I fainted when the host hit my tongue.
And then that nun, who had the statue of Mary that cried tears of blood in the middle of the night (nobody ever saw the statue crying, but the blood collected on a silk cloth that rested beneath) and this cloth, she held it to my forehead to cure me!
It didn't work.

My sister was a nun.

My sister and I would listen to the soundtrack of *Jesus Christ Superstar* all the time and one time she got a crazed look in her eyes and told me she had heard the actor playing Jesus in the movie was actually crucified, killed during the filming. She was twenty-five and I was nine and I used to call her *Sister Sister.* Why would she tell me this? Like some kind of religious snuff film. I've researched it, nothing bad happened on the set of *Jesus Christ Superstar.*

When I get angry, I don't confront someone because I expect people to act appropriately on their own, but also, to avoid confrontation. Since I don't confront them, they keep doing what's making me angry. Then I get so furious I do something impulsive, but covertly. Then I feel guilty. But the angry feeling, the justified anger still conflicts with the guilt in an unresolvable way. It's almost like, by "acting out" when I'm right, instead of confronting the inappropriate person, I wind up being the guilty party instead of the abuser. And if the guilt dissipates, I still haven't had the satisfaction of them being accountable for what they did wrong. I end up paying the price. And that's not right, because they're the ones who did something wrong. As I should take responsibility, they should too. But now it's all weighing me down, and they get to feel wronged.

But I didn't do anything to the wind chime. I left the wind chime alone.

And now I realize it has shifted. I want my own wind chime. From my phone, I google where to buy them. I want a fancy set.

Eventually, I began to doubt everything—I was *basically* sober, but had gone off my antidepressants on my own, obsessed with images of hurting myself physically, fantasies of running through my apartment diving through the window frame, crashing through, head first, or, alternatively, feet first, landing on a spike, again, balancing for a moment on the bone of my carcass, then disemboweling, stuff like that.

And I didn't have health insurance.

So I started taking St. John's wort.

And then I remembered an old prescription for Prozac at Duane Reade! I paid cash for it, I was desperate. Prozac was still weirdly expensive—three hundred and fifty-nine dollars for 30 pills. I went up on the dosage quickly.

One of the things that can happen when you go up on a dose of selective serotonin reuptake inhibitors too quickly is severe constipation, the combination of St. John's wort with the Prozac equaled rocks in my colon. I forced myself to go anyhow—it ripped my ass open—I gave myself a fissure—a tear in the anal lining—which is one of the most painful things one can experience, or so says the medical community, and it turns out this is a common story—went up on Prozac too fast, tore hole in ass, happens all the time, should be a (published) side effect, should be in the "literature."

It felt as if my ass was being stabbed with a knife, and I knew I needed surgery.

Everyone kind of knew the pandemic was coming.

I had been forewarned, but the week before, I finally had the Anal Fistula surgery. I actually had three things going on down there: a skin tag, an anal fistula and a fissure.

I'm tapering down from my off-label high
dosages of Effexor and I go from 375
milligrams to 300 milligrams.
I start to listen to the radio
and it is my sincere feeling that
the radio combined with the
electromagnetic tear in my ass
in turn created a
hole in the space-time continuum.
We have all been transported to 1980
but I can't explain why.
Maybe it's Y2K Maybe it's Zika
Maybe global warming
—or the Montauk Project,
a secret governmental experiment
where the scientists believed
nerves in the sphincters,
when combined with extreme tesla coils,
electromagnetic pulses, and radio transmissions
lead to psychic binding and a tear
in the space-time continuum
for the subject, and everyone
within a 25-foot radius
of the point of insertion
into the anus.
It happened—lots of people missing from public parks.

And now I am at 150 milligrams of Effexor
Thinking
thinking
thinking
thinking
You know
like
hours and hours
a day nonstop since Wednesday
I've just had this breakthrough
and I feel
Really Happy
right now and
I don't think it is an illusional breakthrough but
I'm going to finish up all my projects that are computer-based
and then
in March
I am going to quit my job.

And I am going to work on totally…
you know
step by step
DISENGAGING FROM DOING STUFF WITH COMPUTERS
THAT I USED TO DO IN OTHER WAYS
like writing with a pen on paper
or reading a book
and
I will work
But I am
NOT
GOING TO WORK IN FRONT
OF A
COMPUTER.

So, I'm, I,
that's just going to be my
compass
and stop listening to the radio
on behalf of
the electromagnetic tear in my sphincter
it's going to be exploratory
kind of like a project
I think I'm going to do it.
I wanted to tell you because I am so excited because
I've just been going through
agonizing
agonizing
what am I going to do
what am I going to do
I can't live this life anymore.

Let me clarify—first I got the fissure (tear in anal lining) from the constipation that occurred when I went up too quickly on the anti-depressants. When it healed it left in its wake a skin tag, a little ball of flesh hanging at the former site of the fissure.

But the fissure never did heal completely so that an ongoing micro fissure would come and go, ultimately leaving an anal gland open to infection, so that by the time Covid arrived, I had an anal fistula which is an infected anal gland that has to be completely scraped out surgically in order to heal.

On top of that, the skin tag had to be removed, and the micro fissure, cauterized.

When I arrived at the anal surgeon, I had to get into "position two," leaning over a counter and he literally taped my ass open to get a good look.

You haven't lived until you have had your ass taped open for inspection.

Like bondage tape.

So, I had the surgery.

And I didn't quite know it yet, but Covid was brewing—after the surgery only thing you can do is bathe, I was home, taking Vicodin (which did not cut into the pain but rather changed my relationship to it, and in the end I had to go through withdrawal) and just as I was about to get out of the house, Covid hit, and I couldn't leave—no getting around the pain, or the embarrassment of the reason why, I was consumed with fear I'd re-torn, or that the surgery wouldn't work. I thought, *can I face excruciating anal pain for the rest of my life?*

I became afraid to eat, afraid to shit—the inner workings of my sphincters terrified me—my body, in its most basic functions, had turned against me—it was the ultimate horror movie happening in real time to me. Remember that movie *The Human Centipede* where people are sewn together?

Once I realized so many people were dying, I stopped complaining, and as it got dark, I reclined, like the articles say you are supposed to do. Exist with natural light. But I remember people I work with—the artists with their trust funds, their goddamned grants—having agendas—such ambition—insisting meetings be kept, when in reality the city had come to a halt and was impossible to navigate.

They felt their artistic aspirations trumped a public health emergency, couldn't imagine the idea of the city breaking down.

But so many people did leave to check into hotels.
Couldn't handle being off the grid. Those that left for comfort, I judged them, because there were others who couldn't or didn't have that option.
Ever since then I've felt more vulnerable, society could collapse.
But my ass, the eye of my storm, never better.
It did heal.
I had a great surgeon. I have a new tight beautiful ass.

I met Tattoomuscledad online. In order to meet, he required a letter of introduction—a request for a beating, a formal letter—like something out of Jane Austen or an epistolary novel. And the idea of having to write this letter—this interested me. I submit this letter (I saved it) as Exhibit A as to "Why I No Longer Want to Be a Slave."

Letter to Tattoomuscledad.

Hello Sir.

I'm in the mood to be tortured. It's an odd feeling, but focusing my thoughts and driving me to seek you out to hurt me and then care for me.

Got a good beating on Tuesday night and it has put me in the mood to get more.

A small note after a large orgy.

I am looking for you – someone who likes to inflict pain, to torture.

I've been with this dominant guy who lives in hell's kitchen.

Our time together unfolds like this – he sends me a text – put on combat boots, spandex underwear. I get the restraints, gear, ready. Rings my buzzer, let him in, wait in position, blindfolded – ass up in the air, face in bed. He plays with it, flogging, whipping, but he's left few marks, doesn't do it hard enough, but the setup is hot, I'm blindfolded, don't know what he looks like. He completely objectifies my body and when we are together I do not make a single physical action that is self-motivated nor utter a word not in response to a prompt. He talks about my holes – he's never encountered any like them. This makes me feel special, unique. He lies back, still blindfolded, I give him head, he comes in my mouth, I fall asleep in his arms, his cock in my mouth because I never sleep I am afraid of sleep and dreams – this is the only time I let myself, when I do finally sleep, he sneaks out, like a ghost.

I find it intoxicating, knowing there is visual information occurring most of which is unavailable to me.

When I was little I remember being tied to a tree while we played, "Tickle Dick," and under the gaze of a huge yarn god's eye, my brother kneeling on my

shoulders, spitting. I remember dodge ball, locked in a closet with holes, a broomstick thrust through – a medieval torture device.
I thought it was romantic.
Tuesday night – someone I met online – when he saw the bruises on my ass he went wild, gave me a good satisfying beating.
What he didn't know was how much I can take, and by the end he was hitting me as hard as he could and I was like:
I can't feel it, whatever, are you even doing anything back there.
You know, egging him on…
And he was beating me beating me and finally I broke down crying, at which point he comforted me. Here is a picture of my ass the next day these bruises look better in person much more colorful they have depth and then he sent me on to the next person. Next time I see the dom guy he'll react to the bruises.
I even had bruises on my actual sphincter.
But it didn't hurt very much.

Any mark can set off the next sadist – a roving punching bag – stumbling from place to place – beat by whomever needs it and I train for this – the sheer cardio-vascular effort of travel, pain – I wish I were traveling in a replaceable skeleton. I am transcending, taking in the pain of the world, transforming it, releasing it. This brings me to my fantasy – to be tortured, bruised, pissed on, the things in your profile – I want you to take me out of consciousness.
And what happens while I am out, and where and how I come to are completely up to you.

I sent this letter to Tattoomuscledad and it worked! He agreed to meet me for lunch—I was at work—I stepped out. He ordered me to wear a butt plug and I did, but it kept falling out and as I was headed out the door at work it popped out and created a tent in my shorts. The receptionist asked, "Are you ok?"

In this moment, I thought lunch might be a bad idea, but I was interested—I forced myself—followed.

A fancy upscale diner, Meatpacking district, and he had this thing planned out like Desdemona's handkerchief—he'd drop a bottle of vitamin water, I'd pick it up, keep it, open the door, pull out his chair, let him sit first.

And you and I are thinking: why the vitamin water?

So he dropped it, I picked it up, opened the door, but the vitamin water was a shade of yellowy orange I'd never seen before, and as I was bending over the butt plug falls out again, and I was almost scared it would slip out of my underwear, fall to the ground. But God was on my side because it didn't, it hung in the elastic.

When he told me the vitamin water bottle was filled with piss, "Take a sip," I showed no visible reaction, put it in my backpack, told him I'd save it.

And at this point we were sitting down so I didn't have to worry about the butt plug slipping anymore.

He was a finicky eater—lots of dietary restrictions. And this was when he drops the bomb: He was a member of a leather family of five men into heavy fetishes. There was a pig, a sub-pig, a master, a sir, and a boss, and *I could be the boy! They needed an "Oral Pig Boy."*

What do you do when a man says that to you? Laugh, clearly. And even then I had a steadfast notion I'd always be lost in it—the world—conquered.

I was interested. I don't know about you but I had never heard of a leather family.

I thought of Mormons—sister wives, Idaho—how wonderful it would be—I could turn over my 250 square feet on Ludlow for my own wing in a McMansion.

Maybe the polygamists were onto something.

I wanted to disappear into this completely suburban-sounding leather family—bad shag carpet and a washer dryer—somewhere in deep New Jersey.

Leather couch, flat screen TV.

And when I was bad I'd be kept in the space beneath the porch.

I thought of my normal relationship.

After a while you stop falling in love and just become irritated.

And he told me that meeting me, at this point without permission from above, went against the rules of the leather family—that the master, who lived in Michigan, controls the family—the members all of whom were submissive to Michigan—can't really do *anything* without consulting Michigan—beatings orchestrated via Skype as punishment for breaking these rules. This meeting *must* be kept under wraps. If I wanted to meet him again, I must meet him and the sub-master for an interview to join their family and pretend we had never met heretofore. Tattoomusledad used to be the master, but then he was the sub-pig and his former slave was the sub-master and the guy in Michigan, the master. Tattomuscledad told me he had testicular cancer, also was sore because Michigan had the sub-master taser his balls 15 times, all broadcast on Skype—it really hurt and he felt Michigan was trying to ruin his relationship with the sub-master who used to be his slave (and was, in fact, his longtime lover of 20 years) but he was going with it because Tattoomuscledad and the sub-master lived together and really couldn't afford to separate.

Typical New York real estate story.

But I told him, I had to tell him, that the tasering of his former cancer site, I thought this was mean.

When I thought of Michigan choosing the cancer site as the place of torture—I began to wonder if Michigan may actually be a sadist.

And I was interested.

I took my bottle of piss back to my office and threw it in a drawer and looked forward to my interview, perversely.

I'd haphazardly stumbled across something I couldn't turn away from but it felt like staring into the sun.

I imagined myself splitting in two—leaving one of me behind with the leather family while the real me, the me who went back to work carrying a bottle of yellow vitamin water, his heart drew back at the power of the other's will and its commitment to destruction. And all the while the other me was behind a locked door getting spanked, or beneath my bed, all tangled up in a bag of cuffs, tape, clothespins, shackles. This other me was always behind something.

I found the vitamin water a few months later in my desk drawer and made the mistake of opening it.

Finally, the Leather Family Interview.

That Sunday I went to breakfast with Sir Austin (sub-master), Tattoomuscledad, and although Michigan wasn't present, Sir Austin kept getting up to call him on his cell, and whenever this happened, Tattoomuscledad sat quietly, ashamed? Embarrassed? And in this instance—my bones, my marrow, my intestines—they felt very private to me, but maybe they wouldn't be, if I joined the Leather Family. I was instructed to open doors for them, sit last, let them order for me, eat last.

I am reminded of the Charlotteans—a cotillion-type social dance program for teaching manners I attended when young—the girls wearing gloves, the boys greeting them on the way in, I knowing I was gay and my mom brought me here in the hopes that contact with the other sex, no matter how formal, how twee, how in fact, gay—that this contact would lead to further contact, and I loved it, but for the wrong reasons, and in the end, we would all dance to Lynyrd Skynyrd, Fleetwood Mac, Freebird and boogie on down boogie on down (or could she have sent me here because of the reports the teachers sent home to my parents about my "nasty habits" which involved playing with my balls and smelling my fingers, picking my nose, tweaking my nipples in math—my bad habits of scratching the inside of my ear and then smelling my fingers—could this be why they sent me?). This is where my mind went, not to the future glory of being a member of a leather family but rather to my childhood, me always home, eating Cheetos, Nyquil poured over ice cream, gum rolled in sugar then chewed again, living for the *TV Guide* (obsessively circling what to watch), *Fantasy Island—The Love Boat* (oh look a double episode special). The TV wouldn't die even though it was essentially murder and there was a TV in every room and it was always on.

And in some deep current of my psyche I knew I wasn't done with drugs yet. This wasn't available to me consciously at lunch, but I knew I knew I knew I was worthy of a grander destruction and viciousness of vices, that my destruction should and would be more luxurious than a leather gag and a mouthpiece connected to a toilet—some sort of human urinal.

I waited for everyone to sit down, and then sat down myself, took out my handkerchief, lay it upon my lap, then folded hands, and suddenly felt self-conscious about my clothing choice—tan shorts and a gingham shirt, shaved head but I thought I may have missed a spot, and I looked up to the huge mirror at Balthazar, and imagined it falling, breaking, a shard piercing the jugular of the girl having brunch at the bar with her date—they'd been up all night doing cocaine, they were having oysters, martinis, could barely talk—sunglasses, slurred speech.

In what way was a leather family any different from the typical American family, really, when you took the longer view? They portended to teach me what it means to be in a healthy and committed S&M relationship. But I didn't know, it all felt like mentally ill people clinging to each other through pain. Or like being a 1950s housewife. And I began to wonder if there is such a thing as a healthy S&M relationship. Why couldn't I find someone to just beat the shit out of me, fuck me, and leave?

Sir Austin and Tattoomuscledad had interesting things to say about punishment and torture—how to gut punch with a bruise, how to gut punch without a bruise.

This was all so depressing.

And I wondered, and I hoped, that other tables could hear this conversation.

After another hushed and stuttering cell phone call on an old flip phone, I came to understand that if I were to meet with Tattoomuscledad to play on our own, he would make the rules, but these things would be reported to Michigan and Sir Austin.

Eventually, Sir Austin went to Michigan to spend a week polishing Michigan's leather and ended up seroconverting (Michigan had lied about his HIV status) and after that Michigan dropped off the face of the earth completely—turned out he had a traumatic brain injury causing violent outbursts and disappearing acts, but that all came later and felt tragic, sad—all of this torture and anger an extension or weird symptom of a brain injury, fetishized.

When I finally did get a one-on-one with Tattoomuscledad, it turned out all he wanted was for me to fuck him mercilessly with a dildo for hours—he never came because of the testicular cancer—it went on and on and on until his asshole looked like late Abstract Expressionism, or a wounded Georgia O'Keeffe flower? Finally, he put on a glove and stuck one finger up my ass for one second. That was it.

And in retrospect all I can think of is the seroconversion, and not to mention Sir Austin asking me if I knew where to get some Special K, that *there is nothing like being fisted on K*, and I said, "I'm sober but give me fifty bucks and a cab voucher and I'll get you whatever you want." What's wrong with these people who can't find drugs for themselves? So much for wanting to be a slave.

And this makes me think of politics. And counterphobia which is a response to anxiety that, instead of fleeing the source of fear in the manner of a phobia, actively seeks it out, in the hope of overcoming the original anxiousness, seeking out what is feared. When I get back from my walk, I wash my hands and then immediately go online and buy five wind chimes.

In the mirror, I look skinny, too skinny, and grungy and haggard, with that expression that you get in your eyes when you are exhausted and everything is like a dream and you are beginning to understand what things are like underneath what people say they are.

Please God, forgive me for anticipating other people's needs.

I sense my soul leaving my body.

Forgive me for trying to please others instead of myself and forgive me for blaming others for the spot I am in now.

I leapt in with no inclined or ready friends about and when I plunged I plummeted to the sound of loud chuckling.

Forgive me for feeling anxiety and guilt when other people have bigger problems than mine.

You are a reflection of my own guilt.

Am I a monster, or is this what it feels like to be human?

You are rubber and you are real.

I think I want to put a wind chime on my own fire escape.

Let us pray.

I went to a bar and cruised a man with muscles. Turns out I knew his roommate, fed him steak when he was sick and couldn't cook. He asked me what I do, I told him I work for a writer. He thought I said I work for Ryder, as in rent-a-truck. Just as well, I thought, and I eased into my new profession. Ryder has a branch across the street, I told him I just came in from work. I concocted a job entailing driving trucks through all the states, delivering and filling them, making sure each branch has enough. He asked me if I have an uncut cock, he had a fetish, you see, and that's what he was looking for. I decided the charade had gone on long enough, I am cut, I confessed, but I wish I weren't. I can't remember that bit of flesh, that part of me that's already dead, disintegrated. Too bad it was not still alive, we could graft it to my gums. I'm not your man, I told him. He said goodbye and I was jealous of his knowing what he wanted and where to find it. He went into the bathroom for a long time. I figured he was opting for non-verbal communication. This way he could strike it up after he knew the condition of their skin. I decided he's got a good system, a scam, and I respect this type of thinking, planning, I was flattered he took the extra time to talk to me. He could have waited until I had to pee.

I imagined myself with an uncut cock, driving a Ryder truck to Mississippi, smoking cigarettes, listening to the radio with him at my side, pouring water out of a jug and handing it to me while I drove. We'd have the air-conditioning on high, with the windows open wide, eating peaches, making small talk on the CB, basking in the comfort of knowing where we were going.

Acknowledgments

For B. E.

With thanks to Alan Felsenthal, Ben Estes, Joe Westmoreland, Eileen Myles, Charlie Kaufman, Robert Glück, Michelle Tea, Lydia Eccles, Lia Gangitano, John Azzopardi, MacDowell, and The Edward F. Albee Foundation.

OTHER TITLES FROM THE SONG CAVE:

1. *A Dark Dreambox of Another Kind* by **Alfred Starr Hamilton**
2. *My Enemies* by **Jane Gregory**
3. *Rude Woods* by **Nate Klug**
4. *Georges Braque and Others* by **Trevor Winkfield**
5. *The Living Method* by **Sara Nicholson**
6. *Splash State* by **Todd Colby**
7. *Essay Stanzas* by **Thomas Meyer**
8. *Illustrated Games of Patience* by **Ben Estes**
9. *Dark Green* by **Emily Hunt**
10. *Honest James* by **Christian Schlegel**
11. *M* by **Hannah Brooks-Motl**
12. *What the Lyric Is* by **Sara Nicholson**
13. *The Hermit* by **Lucy Ives**
14. *The Orchid Stories* by **Kenward Elmslie**
15. *Do Not Be a Gentleman When You Say Goodnight* by **Mitch Sisskind**
16. *HAIRDO* by **Rachel B. Glaser**
17. *Motor Maids across the Continent* by **Ron Padgett**
18. *Songs for Schizoid Siblings* by **Lionel Ziprin**
19. *Professionals of Hope: The Selected Writings of* **Subcomandante Marcos**
20. *Fort Not* by **Emily Skillings**
21. *Riddles, Etc.* by **Geoffrey Hilsabeck**
22. *CHARAS: The Improbable Dome Builders* by **Syeus Mottel** (Co-published with Pioneer Works)
23. *YEAH NO* by **Jane Gregory**
24. *Nioque of the Early-Spring* by **Francis Ponge**

25. *Smudgy and Lossy* by **John Myers**

26. *The Desert* by **Brandon Shimoda**

27. *Scardanelli* by **Friederike Mayröcker**

28. *The Alley of Fireflies and Other Stories* by **Raymond Roussel**

29. *CHANGES: Notes on Choreography* by **Merce Cunningham**
(Co-published with the Merce Cunningham Trust)

30. *My Mother Laughs* by **Chantal Akerman**

31. *Earth* by **Hannah Brooks-Motl**

32. *Everything and Other Poems* by **Charles North**

33. *Paper Bells* by **Phan Nhiên Hạo**

34. *Photographs: Together & Alone* by **Karlheinz Weinberger**

35. *A Better Place Is Hard to Find* by **Aaron Fagan**

36. *Rough Song* by **Blanca Varela**

37. *In the Same Light: 200 Poems for Our Century From the Migrants & Exiles of the Tang Dynasty*, translated by **Wong May**

38. *On the Mesa: An Anthology of Bolinas Writing (50th Anniversary Edition)*, edited by **Ben Estes and Joel Weishaus**

39. *Listen My Friend, This Is the Dream I Dreamed Last Night* by **Cody-Rose Clevidence**

40. *Poetries* by **Georges Schehadé**

41. *Wings in Time* by **Callie Garnett**

42. *Two Murals* by **Jesús Castillo**

43. *Punks: New & Selected Poems* by **John Keene**

44. *ABC Moonlight* by **Ben Estes**

45. *Star Lake* by **Arda Collins**

46. *The Maybe-Bird* by **Jennifer Elise Foerster**

47. *Seriously Well* by **Helge Torvund**

48. *Dereliction* by **Gabrielle Octavia Rucker**

49. *Bookworm: Conversations with* **Michael Silverblatt**

50. *April* by **Sara Nicholson**

51. *Valley of the Many-Colored Grasses* by **Ronald Johnson**

52. *The Sphinx and the Milky Way: Selections from the Notebooks of* **Charles Burchfield**

53. *Telling the Truth as It Comes Up: Selected Talks & Essays 1991–2018* by **Alice Notley**

54. *Lunar Solo: Selected Poems* by **Jules Laforgue**

55. *Stranger* by **Emily Hunt**

56. *The Selkie* by **Morgan Võ**

57. *Hereafter* by **Alan Felsenthal**

58. *Cold Dogs* by **Zan de Parry**

59. *Saturday* by **Margaret Ross**

60. *Many Poems* by **Roberta Iannamico**

61. *Ultraviolet of the Genuine* by **Hannah Brooks-Motl**

62. *Silkworm's Pansori* by **David Seung**

63. *Tantrums in Air* by **Emily Skillings**

64. *Jump Cuts: Essays on Surrealism, Film, Music, Culture, and Other Utopian Topics* by **Mark Polizzotti**

65. *Earthly: Selected Poems* by **Jean Follain**

66. *Nebraska* by **George Whitmore**

67. *Behind the State Capitol: Or Cincinnati Pike* by **John Wieners**

68. *PACES THE CAGE* by **S*an D. Henry-Smith**

69. *Shake Until Cloudy* by **Amanda Nadelberg**

70. *Shit Hike* by **Callie Garnett**

71. *Writing a Letter: Akerman Ballet, Act One* by **Collier Schorr**